Lizzie McGUiRE

Lizzie for PRESIDENT

Adapted by Alice Alfonsi
Based on the series created by Terri Minsky
Part One is based on a teleplay written
by Melissa Gould.
Part Two is based on a teleplay written
by Douglas Tuber & Tim Maile.

Watch it on

DISNEY CHANNEL

abc Kids

DISNEY PRESS

VOLO

New York

Printed in the United States of America

First Edition
1 3 5 7 9 10 8 6 4 2

Library of Congress Catalog Card Number: 2003112306

ISBN 0-7868-4632-1
For more Disney Press fun, visit www.disneybooks.com
Visit DisneyChannel.com

PART ONE

CHAPTER ONE

Something was definitely up.

The Hillridge Junior High cheerleaders were being nice—and not just to the jocks. The pom-pom princesses were talking to every kid they passed in the cafeteria, regardless of their dorkiness level.

"Hey! Hi!" said Kate Sanders, smiling at Harvey Barnes, a Mathlete with acne issues. The poor kid almost fainted from shock.

"Hi, nice to meet you!" Claire Miller gushed to Janice Baxter, a shy, gawky girl who was secretary of the Audiovisual Club.

Before today, Claire never even *glanced* at an "uncool" person like Janice. Now she was treating the girl like a long-lost cousin . . . or a *sibling* even!

Time for a reality check, Lizzie McGuire thought. She leaned toward her best friend, Miranda Sanchez, who was sitting across from her at their usual lunchroom table. "Okay, something's going on. Claire is being nice—to *everybody*—and Kate's not even stopping her."

Miranda nodded. "Tell me about it. She actually said hi to *me* this morning."

Lizzie watched Kate and Claire continue their gushfest, from table to table, all the way across the cafeteria. This was totally unbelievable. The Hillridge cafeteria wasn't just some big, uncharted landmass where you ate your lunch. It was a region with very specific territories. There was Cool-ville, Normal Land,

and at least three levels of Dorkdom. And Kate and Claire were doing the unthinkable—crossing every single border! When they reached the corner table against the back wall, Lizzie's jaw dropped.

"Claire is talking to the dorkestra!" Lizzie blurted.

Claire, the witchiest snob in school, was giving props to a girl who carried her lunch around in a violin case! And Kate was practically flirting with Felix Martin, a kid who once had a piece of sheet music taped to his back for three entire periods before he even noticed!

"They must've lost a dare," Miranda said.

Lizzie wasn't so sure. And then, her other best friend, David "Gordo" Gordon, sat down with his lunch tray and cleared it all up.

"This just in," he reported. "Claire is running for class president."

"No wonder," said Lizzie.

"It's so unfair," said Miranda. "Claire's going to end up our class president, and it's only because she's popular."

"The popular kids win everything," Lizzie said with a sigh. "It's been that way since kindergarten. The rest of us are just doomed."

As Miranda nodded in agreement, something caught her eye. Her eyebrows rose, and her features scrunched up into an expression of confusion and horror. "Uhm, you guys? Why is Larry Tudgeman eating *worms*?"

Lizzie and Gordo followed Miranda's gaze to a table deep in the land of Dorkdom. Two kids were staring at Larry, who was dangling a worm close to his open mouth.

"Oh, Larry's running, too," Gordo explained with a shrug. "He said he'd eat one worm for every person who votes for him."

Lizzie shuddered as Larry dropped the

squirming earthworm into his mouth. Why was Tudgeman always such a . . . *Tudgeman*!

Miranda grimaced. "That's kind of desperate. Not to mention gross."

"And very unfair to the worms," Lizzie pointed out.

"Great choice," said Gordo rolling his eyes in disgust. "Claire or Tudgeman." Then he thought about it a moment and said, "Why doesn't anyone *normal* run? Like us."

"One of *us* run?" Miranda put her hand on Gordo's forehead. "Are you feeling okay?"

"It could work. We're not popular, but we don't *need* to be. We are . . . the normals!" Gordo declared.

Lizzie looked at Miranda, then at Gordo. *Huh?*

"There are more of us than there are of them," he explained, getting more excited by the second. "If we can just get everyone to vote for a *normal* candidate, we could win!"

"You think?" Miranda asked hopefully.

Gordo nodded enthusiastically.

Wow, thought Lizzie. Gordo is really on to something!

Yeah, let's overthrow the ruling powers!

"Which is why I nominate *you*, Lizzie McGuire!" Gordo announced.

Lizzie's eyes widened in shock. "Me?"

Miranda blinked. It took her a second to get used to the idea, but once she did, she said, "He's right. You're like *totally* normal."

Lizzie frowned at Miranda.

"That's a good thing," Miranda assured her.

"You guys are joking," said Lizzie. "I am not . . . am I?"

"You have what it takes," said Gordo. "You're one of the normals. *You* could be our class president!"

"You could be . . . the voice of the people!" said Miranda, with her hand extended dramatically as if she were presenting Lizzie to her adoring public.

The voice of the people, Lizzie repeated to herself. That actually sounded kind of cool—not to mention the idea of an adoring public.

Suddenly, Lizzie saw herself running for higher office. Representative Lizzie McGuire . . . Senator Lizzie McGuire . . . President of the United States—Lizzie McGuire . . . For a second, she actually wondered if Mount Rushmore had enough room for one more face.

"Okay, I'll do it," Lizzie told her friends,

suddenly sure of herself. "I *will* run for class president!"

Of course, once she'd actually *said* it, she suddenly *wasn't* so sure anymore.

i don't have a good feeling about this.

CHAPTER TWO

"**O**ur daughter," said Mr. McGuire at breakfast the next morning. "The voice of the people."

He gazed proudly at Lizzie, who was sitting at the kitchen table, trying to scarf down her cereal and get the heck out from under her parents' annoying, well-meaning thumbs, like, as soon as possible.

"You know," Mr. McGuire went on, "I was president of the Audiovisual Club."

Lizzie could just imagine her dad's geeky photo in his old yearbook. It wasn't really a part of her genetic code that she wanted to dwell on.

"Uh, I'm sure you were, Dad," she said. "Anyway, Gordo thinks we may actually have a chance at winning the election."

"I knew you were destined for greatness the day you were born," Lizzie's mom declared. She was standing at the counter, making Lizzie's lunch. "I'm gifted that way. Just like I knew that guy on *Survivor* was going to win."

Okay, so Mom's a little out there. Gotta love her, though. i mean, look at the way she still cuts the crusts off my PB & J.

Just then, Lizzie's seriously toxic little brother ran into the kitchen and grabbed two cereal bowls.

"Hey," Mrs. McGuire shouted. "One bowl's enough, mister."

Matt ignored her. He took the two bowls to the table and sat down. Then he put one bowl in front of himself and the other bowl in front of the empty seat beside him.

Mr. McGuire didn't care about the cereal bowls. He was more concerned about Matt's being late for the bus to elementary school. "Nice of you to show your face, Matt," he said, pointing to his wristwatch.

"Well, it's not my fault!" Matt cried. "Jasper keeps hiding my shoes."

"Who's Jasper?" asked Mrs. McGuire.

"And what does he want with your shoes?" asked Lizzie. "Is he all out of *stink*?"

Suddenly, the telephone rang. Lizzie lunged

for it, totally grateful for the excuse to bolt from this lame conversation. "It's probably Gordo. I'll take it upstairs!"

With Lizzie gone, Matt was sitting alone at the kitchen table. But Lizzie's little brother didn't *act* like he was alone. He turned to the empty chair next to him, jerked his thumb in the direction from which Lizzie had just fled, and said, "*That's* the girl I was telling you about. She claims to be human, but I beg to differ."

Mr. and Mrs. McGuire watched their son address the empty chair.

"Who are you talking to, kiddo?" asked Mrs. McGuire.

Matt rolled his eyes. "Jasper!" he said. "My new friend I was telling you about."

"Your new friend, huh?" said Mr. McGuire. "Well, why don't you tell me *where* your new friend *is*, Matt?"

"Don't be a doof, Dad," said Matt. Then he

turned toward the empty chair again and said, "Must be something in the water. My whole family's kind of—"

Matt twirled his finger near his temple making the universal sign for "gone totally insane."

Mr. and Mrs. McGuire gawked at the empty chair. Neither was quite sure what to do or say next.

"Mom, Dad, don't stare at him like that!" cried Matt. "It's not his fault his mom gives him funny haircuts."

Then Matt jumped up. "We'll take these to go!" he declared, grabbing both bowls of cereal and dashing out.

"Isn't our son a little bit *old* to have an imaginary friend?" Mr. McGuire asked his wife.

Mrs. McGuire shook her head. "I *knew* we got off too easy when he potty-trained so early."

* * *

Meanwhile, upstairs, a typical three-way call was underway between Lizzie and her two best friends.

"I cannot believe I'm running for class president against Claire," Lizzie told Gordo and Miranda.

"Well, you may not have her talent, and you may not have her charm," said Gordo. "And she does have that great smile—"

"Yeah, yeah, Gordo," said Lizzie, cutting him off. "I *get* the point."

Lizzie checked herself out in the mirror across the room. She'd pulled a section of her blond hair into a high ponytail and secured it with three sparkly mini-scrunchies. Her red-print capri pants and lotus-flower top looked cute, too.

Good hair day: check.

Cute outfit: check.

Lizzie was ready for just about anything now.

"Look, people want to see a change," Gordo told her, "and that's why you can win."

"And when he says 'see a change,' he doesn't mean Claire's *wardrobe*," Miranda pointed out. "She's the only girl at school who reaccessorizes between classes!"

"Got it," Lizzie told Miranda. "See you guys at school."

"Bye," said Gordo and Miranda at the same time. Then they all hung up.

I can't believe it, thought Lizzie. I actually have a campaign staff. "This is so *West Wing*!" she said dreamily.

"Oh, Miranda, the posters look great!" said Lizzie as she walked down the school hallway with her friends later that morning.

"They do, don't they?" said Miranda, proud of her work.

The posters were really eye-catching, with orange and red flames licking the totally inspiring campaign slogan: MCGUIRE'S ON FIRE!

"They're broad and nonspecific," Gordo said in his no-nonsense campaign manager's voice. "Claire's are all made out of footballs and pom-poms. Original, but alienating. We're off to a good start."

"Maybe," said Lizzie. "But is Larry really serious about those worms?"

The three had passed Tudgeman on their way to Lizzie's locker. He was wearing his usual stained putty-colored shirt with the lime green collar, and he'd set up a table with a big poster that displayed his own slogan: I'LL EAT A WORM IF YOU VOTE FOR ME. On his table was that disgusting bucket of earthworms he'd been carrying around for three days!

Unfortunately, the stunt had actually attracted a few kids.

But how many of the worms had he eaten exactly? Gordo felt this was a critical campaign question. So he'd given Miranda the task of snooping out the answer.

"So far he's consumed five," Miranda reported.

Gordo tapped his chin, pondering a strategy for his candidate. "Tudgeman's all about shocking people," he told Lizzie. "Think of him as Marilyn Manson to your Britney Spears."

Lizzie nodded. Sure, I'll be Britney, she thought. That's cool with me.

"Just remember," Gordo added, "be normal."

Lizzie nodded again, then noticed Claire and Kate walking toward her.

As usual, Claire was wearing her cheerleader uniform and Kate was dressed in a superpolished designer outfit complete with a little pearl necklace. Also as usual, their smiles were as fake as AstroTurf.

"Lizzie McGuire. My little opponent," said Claire, all superior.

"Hi, Claire. Kate," said Lizzie flatly.

"Loser!" cried Kate, making her thumb and forefinger into an L and shaking it in front of Lizzie's face.

What a witch! thought Lizzie.

"Just wanted to tell you how *cute* I think it is that you think you actually have a *chance* against me," said Claire.

"Cute in a *loser* kind of way," added Kate.

Lizzie shrunk back from Claire and Kate who were in total she-beast mode, trying to intimidate her. Lizzie really wanted to say something back, but she was at a total loss. She looked to Gordo. *Help!*

And help he did. Gordo stepped right up to Claire and Kate. "Look," he said, "Lizzie McGuire's the voice of the people, and there are more of us than there are of you, which makes hers the voice of the *winner.* That's what Lizzie always says."

"I do?" Lizzie whispered.

"You *will,*" said Gordo, taking a piece of folded notebook paper out of his pocket. "It's all in this speech I've written for you."

Lizzie took the paper and looked it over. *Cool!*

Claire didn't like that Gordo was answering for Lizzie—especially since he'd answered so *well.* So, she shoved her palm in front of his face.

"She's giving you the hand!" Miranda gasped to Gordo in horror.

"Bottom line, I'm popular," Claire said directly to Lizzie, "and you're not, so I win."

Lizzie gulped. She *had* to answer now, but what should she say?

Gordo turned to her. "Don't you remember our phone conversation this morning?"

Lizzie nodded.

"You're powerful! You're normal!" he reminded her. "Go!"

Lizzie swallowed her nerves and took a step toward Claire. "Let me tell you something, Miss Claire Witch Project!"

"Ooh! Good one!" squealed Miranda.

"I may not be cheerleader captain, and I may not be yearbook editor, and I may not sit in the cool part of the cafeteria. But people want to see change and—no, no, no—I'm not talking about your *wardrobe*."

Claire actually winced at *that* one!

"Yeah!" said Miranda.

"So laugh all you want to now," Lizzie continued, "'cause by the end of this thing, you'll be crying."

Hey, who was that? Wait, that was me! Not bad . . . I think.

Claire looked at Kate. But neither of them could think of a thing to say to that. *Exiting* was the only strategy they could come up with! So they did. *Real* fast.

"You're a quick study, Lizzie McGuire," said Gordo proudly as he watched the well-groomed she-beasts flee.

"Excuse me, Lizzie?" asked a small voice.

Lizzie, Gordo, and Miranda turned to find Veruca Albano standing in front of them with her usual stack of library books.

Veruca wore glasses and often did her hair in a strange, antifashion three-braid style that sort of resembled abstract art. She was also the president of the Mathlete Club—and a proud citizen of the land of she-geeks.

"Veruca. Hi," said Lizzie.

"I just saw you stand up to Claire," said Veruca with a big smile. "And I want to let you know that you'll get the vote of the Mathletes."

"That's nine votes!" noted Gordo.

Nine votes, *pour moi* . . . ? They like me—they really, really like me!

CHAPTER THREE

The presidential campaign was off and running.

After lunch the next day, on the school's grassy quad, Lizzie held a rally. A small group of student protesters surrounded her. Some held signs with photos of frogs and the words BE NICE, DON'T SLICE.

"Frog dissection should be optional!" Lizzie declared to the crowd. "We should be allowed to exercise our free will and write a paper instead!"

The protesters cheered.

Standing in the back, Lizzie's campaign team watched—and worked. Miranda was counting up potential votes. And Gordo was thinking about which student group Lizzie should address next.

"My plan is to find a better way," Lizzie told the group. "And for that, I'll need your involvement!"

Lizzie looked toward Gordo. He gestured for her to keep going. So Lizzie continued.

"Friends and fellow students, I think it is time to ask not what your student government can do for you—ask what you can do for your student government!"

The group went wild. "Be nice, don't slice! Be nice, don't slice!" they chanted.

Some of the crowd even started chanting, "Lizzie! Lizzie! Lizzie!"

At the back of the crowd, Miranda nodded. "Great speech," she remarked.

"Thanks," said Gordo.

Miranda squinted at Gordo. *Huh?*

"*I* wrote it," he explained.

The next day, as Lizzie passed out flyers on her way to class, Gordo continued to advise her.

"People are watching your every move," he said. "So when you're in the language labs, you speak Spanish, you speak French, you speak Italian. When in Home Ec, you cook, you sew, you mend. When in Gym, you rebound, you go the extra distance, you run like the wind."

Just then, Lizzie noticed a big kid hassling a smaller one.

"Gimme your lunch money, you little twerp!" demanded the bully.

Even though Lizzie didn't know these two, she figured this was just the sort of situation a good candidate should get involved in. She turned to Gordo. "What do I do?"

Gordo shuffled through his Campaign Strategies index cards until he found the one he wanted.

"The Cost of Lunch speech," he said. "Here!" Gordo shoved the card at Lizzie— and she bolted toward the bully and his victim.

Lizzie stumbled slightly, then regained her balance and cleared her throat. "Excuse me!" she said, "The price of lunch *is* a bit high, isn't it? Vote for me, Lizzie McGuire, and I can promise you I will do something about it."

The bully, who was now rifling through the smaller kid's jacket pockets, turned toward Lizzie.

"Can you hold on a second, please," he told her. Then he turned back to the geeky kid and gave him a wedgie.

Yikes!

"Now—you were saying?" the bully asked Lizzie.

Lizzie glared at Gordo. *Is this really going to work?*

Gordo obviously thought so. He gestured to Lizzie, encouraging her to keep going. A vote was a vote, after all. And if she could distract the bully, his victim could make a hasty exit.

"Walk with me!" she told the bully.

Gordo watched them go, pleased and impressed.

Over the next week, the race for class president really heated up—and so did the campaigning.

"Lizzie McGuire, voice of the people!" Miranda declared as she passed out flyers in the quad every day. "McGuire's on Fire. Vote for Lizzie!"

Unfortunately, Larry Tudgeman was in the quad every day, too. Eating worms.

"Go, go, go, go, go!" five football players chanted as Tudgeman ate five worms in a row.

Shuddering with disgust, Miranda looked the other way. Only the king of all science geeks would turn a presidential campaign into an experiment in human digestion, Miranda thought.

Lizzie was hard at work earning votes, too. But not by eating worms. She was busy visiting every student group on Gordo's long list.

In the language lab one day, she addressed a group of foreign exchange students from a variety of countries. Lizzie wasn't so great at foreign languages, so Gordo stood in the back of the room, holding up giant flash cards for her.

"Bonjour!" read Lizzie.

The French-speaking kids clapped, and Gordo nodded approvingly.

He held up another flash card for Lizzie.

"*Hola!*" said Lizzie.

Now the Spanish-speaking kids applauded.

A third card went up.

"*Shalom,*" said Lizzie.

The kids who spoke Hebrew applauded.

Score! thought Lizzie. She'd gotten applause from every single foreign exchange student!

The next day, Lizzie posed for a picture with the Mathletes. To show her solidarity with *them*, she'd worn her hair like Veruca— with three braids popping out at odd angles.

Next, Lizzie visited the Science Fiction Club. Gordo told Lizzie if she dressed up like a *Star Wars* character, she was sure to get their votes. So she did—even though she felt like a total dork having Princess Leia cinnamon-bun braids plastered to the sides of her head.

Since there were *Star Trek* fans in the club, too, Gordo had to think of something that would make *them* happy. From the back of the room, he held up his hand so Lizzie could see how to position her fingers correctly in the traditional Vulcan greeting. Very Mr. Spock!

Lizzie contorted her hand into the correct position, and the sci-fi club cheered.

Score again! thought Lizzie. This showing-your-solidarity-to-earn-votes thing is really working!

CHAPTER FOUR

After a week of campaigning, things were looking quite positive. "I knew my plan to beat the popular kids would work!" Gordo told Lizzie and Miranda as they walked to lunch.

"Guess I really am the voice of the people," Lizzie said with pride.

"The election's not over yet," Miranda reminded her in a "don't count your votes until they're tallied" tone.

Miranda had been doing a lot of intelligence gathering—aka *snooping*—and she knew the competition was fierce. "Tudgeman's not that far behind," she warned Lizzie, "and I saw him digging for worms before school."

Gross, thought Lizzie.

i would *never* swallow worms for votes!

"You don't have to worry about Tudgeman," said Gordo as they filed into the lunch line and picked up their plastic trays. "He went to the nurse's office, complaining of stomach cramps. And Claire hasn't even infiltrated the Drama Groupies."

The Drama Groupies were a club of about

ten kids who wore black outfits and dark sunglasses on a regular basis. Theater, foreign films, and New York City were their main topics of conversation. They were cool. Not cheerleader/jock cool, of course, but running a not-so-distant second.

"But the Drama Club is, like, second-tier *popular*," Miranda told Gordo. "Which means they're going to vote for Claire."

"Not if I can get them to vote for *me*," Lizzie said, feeling superconfident in her ability to make any group think she was really one of them. She'd already talked over a Drama Groupies strategy with Gordo.

When the three friends had reached their lunch table, Gordo gave Lizzie her usual "pre-political appearance" pep talk.

"Okay, Lizzie," he said, "we've gone over this. You know what to do. You have to blend, but don't smile. Drama Groupies don't smile."

"I can do this, Gordo," she assured him.

"Lizzie McGuire, you've become everything I hoped for and more!" gushed Gordo. "A chameleon, changing colors whenever necessary at precisely the right moment. It scares me how good you are." He grinned with pride.

But Lizzie frowned.

She was less than thrilled to have her behavior compared to a reptile's.

Somehow, that doesn't sound better than swallowing worms.

"I can't believe I'm about to go hang with the Drama Club," said Lizzie, psyching up for the task at hand.

"But you're *not*," snapped Miranda. "You

said you'd have lunch with the Foreign Exchange Club. They've even made you food from their homelands."

Lizzie held up her hands, palms toward the ceiling. "Foreign Exchange Club mystery meat?" she said, weighing down one hand, as if it were one half of a butcher's scale. "Or cool Drama Club?" she said, weighing down the other hand.

She turned her hands over, as if emptying both of them. "I think I'm going with the Drama Club."

"But you promised them!" said Miranda.

"Just tell them I've been campaigning so hard, I need the time to catch up on my homework."

"But that would be a *lie*," said Miranda.

"You call it a lie—I call it politics," said Lizzie with a shrug. "Tell her, Gordo," she added, tossing her hair over her shoulder.

No, Miranda's right. it's a lie!

Both girls waited for Gordo to say something. He seemed to be thinking it over.

"Gordo!" cried Lizzie and Miranda together.

"The Drama Club's a very influential group, Miranda," Gordo finally said in his calm Mr. Logic voice. "If Lizzie's seen with them at lunch, there's no telling how many more votes we'll get. Who she's seen with is very important."

Miranda was dumbfounded. Before this whole election thing started, Gordo was all about being real, and standing by your word, and not compromising your principles.

Was he really dumping everything he'd

once believed in just to win a stupid school election?

"Gordo, she's known about this lunch since yesterday!" argued Miranda.

But Miranda's words were wasted. As far as Lizzie was concerned, if Gordo was defending her decision, then that was that.

"See, I told you. It's politics," Lizzie said to Miranda with a shrug. "Gordo?"

Gordo slid Lizzie the pair of sunglasses he'd been carrying around in his shirt pocket. She put them on. Next, he held up a black leather jacket. She slipped her arms into it.

After tossing her friends a "Later," and a little half-wave, Lizzie was off.

Miranda and Gordo watched their best friend leave Normal Land and head for Coolville.

With confidence, Lizzie strode up to the Drama Groupies' table. The kids, dressed in black, paused from their conversations to check her out. A few slid their sunglasses down their noses.

Lizzie cocked her hip and said something cool, and a few kids in the group invited her to join them.

The little scene made Gordo unbelievably happy. And Miranda unbelievably sorry she'd gotten involved in this election thing in the first place.

"What has gotten into her?" she asked Gordo.

"I don't know," he said with a grin. "But whatever it is, it's making me all tingly inside."

If looks could kill, Miranda's would have at least sent Gordo to the hospital.

CHAPTER FIVE

In the grassy backyard of the McGuire house, Matt swung his bat once, twice, three times.

The baseballs were being thrown at him one after the other. But they weren't coming from a human pitcher. They were coming from an expensive ball-pitching machine. A brand-new one.

Mr. and Mrs. McGuire had surprised Matt with it when he got home from school an hour ago. Now they stood on the deck, watching their son enjoy himself.

"Wow!" cried Mrs. McGuire when Matt connected with one of the balls. "Good."

"Nice one, son," said Mr. McGuire as he hit another.

"This is great!" said Matt, taking another swing. "And it's not even my birthday! Thanks, Mom. Thanks, Dad."

Up on the deck, Mrs. McGuire turned to her husband. "It's working," she whispered.

Mr. McGuire nodded. "He hasn't even mentioned his little invisible friend."

Suddenly, Matt stopped swinging. He walked over to the deck, pulled off his batting helmet, and sat down on a step, his shoulders hunched in a defeated posture.

Mr. and Mrs. McGuire shared a concerned look.

"Sweetie? Something wrong?" asked Mrs. McGuire.

"It's just . . . on Jasper's planet, baseball is evil," Matt said.

"Well, it may be time for you and Jasper to go your separate ways," said Mr. McGuire gently. "Perhaps you've outgrown each other."

"Yeah, you know, it happens to the best of friends sometimes," said Mrs. McGuire.

"It does," echoed Mr. McGuire.

"You guys!" said Matt in a loud whisper. "Jasper can *hear* you! You're hurting his feelings."

Mr. and Mrs. McGuire glanced at each other worriedly. Apparently, the expensive ball-pitching machine hadn't worked after all. Their son was still acting like a crazy boy.

"You know, Matt," said Mrs. McGuire, "what Dad and I are trying to say is that, uh . . . hey! Where's the old gang?"

"Yeah," said Mr. McGuire, nodding.

"We haven't seen them around much lately," added Mrs. McGuire.

"That's 'cause they're way into their video games," said Matt with a dejected shrug. Suddenly, he brightened. "Did you know that Jasper's parents were snowmen?"

Mrs. McGuire swallowed nervously. "Snowmen? Oh. Wow."

"So if we were to get you that video dream thing," said Mr. McGuire, recalling the hot, new—not to mention, *expensive*—video game system he'd seen in commercials, like, a *zillion* times recently, "then maybe you could start hanging out with some of your real—"

Mrs. McGuire nudged him in the ribs.

"—real *old* friends, again?" finished Mr. McGuire, rubbing his side.

Matt shrugged. "Guess so."

Mr. McGuire stared off into space. "That'd be okay with you, wouldn't it, Jasper?"

Mrs. McGuire followed her husband's lead. "Yeah, Jasper, you wouldn't mind, would you?"

Matt frowned. "Jasper flew away!" he informed them testily.

"Oh," said Mr. McGuire. But the look he gave his wife said something else: unless we find a way to make "Jasper" fly away for good, *I'm* going to be the resident crazy boy!

Across town, at the Digital Bean cybercafe, Lizzie was hangin' with Miranda and Gordo.

Gordo could really feel the tension between Lizzie and Miranda. So, when Lizzie asked him to get her a drink, he was glad to get up from the table.

When he came back, he handed Lizzie a bottle of apple juice. She scrunched up her face, like she was annoyed.

"Apple juice from *concentrate*?" she said. "I was kind of hoping for fresh squeezed."

Okay, when is someone going to stop me?

"You don't *squeeze* apples," said Gordo. "You core, peel, and crush them."

"Fine," snapped Lizzie, reaching for it. "I'll drink it."

"No, no, you're right," said Gordo, grabbing it back. "You've been working real hard, campaigning like crazy. Well, at least as hard as Tudgeman over there."

Apparently, the trip to the nurse's office had only slowed the Tudge down temporarily. Yet another group of kids had surrounded him with cries of "Gross!" "Ew!" and "Just got my vote!"

Gordo sighed and asked Lizzie, "What can I get you instead of the apple juice?"

Lizzie considered her options. She noticed a few Drama Groupies in a cozy corner of the Bean, holding huge, steaming mugs of coffee.

That looked like a good thing to drink—and, more important, a *cool* thing to drink. The perfect drink for her "class president" image.

"Coffee. Three creams," she told Gordo.

Coffee?!

Miranda gasped, but Gordo didn't.

"Coffee," he said, nodding. "I like it. It's sophisticated—it's edgy. I'll be right back."

After Gordo was out of earshot, Miranda turned to Lizzie. "Since when are you on the bean?" she snapped.

"The Drama Club is drinking coffee, so *I'm* drinking coffee," Lizzie said, all superior.

"But coffee stains your teeth, stunts your growth, and gives you bad breath," Miranda pointed out.

Lizzie used to rattle off these very same facts herself—before she'd turned into a political creature, more concerned with her *image* than just about anything else.

"And why is Gordo taking your drink order?" continued Miranda.

"Because Gordo understands," said Lizzie with a shrug. "I can't stand in line with everyone."

"Are you, like, Claire's twin or something?" Miranda asked, narrowing her eyes.

"Things are changing," said Lizzie with a little sneer. "You really ought to try and keep up."

"Oh, I can," said Miranda. "I'm just choosing not to." Miranda stood up. Little Miss Candidate had finally gone too far.

As Gordo returned with Lizzie's coffee, Miranda told him, "Way to go Dr. Frankenstein. You've just created a monster."

Then Miranda stomped off.

Lizzie just rolled her eyes.

"She'll come around," said Gordo.

Lizzie wasn't worried. She took the dramatic-looking coffee cup from Gordo. With a glance back up at the Drama Groupies in the corner, she took a big sip—and spit it out.

"Gordo. I said *three* creams," she snapped. "And this tastes like two!"

Her tone was so superior, Gordo was taken aback for a second. He stared at Lizzie and wondered for the first time if maybe Miranda was right.

But all he said was, "I'll, uh, get you another."

After Gordo left, Lizzie waved at one of the Drama Groupies, who waved back. Sticking out her thumb and pinkie like a phone receiver, Lizzie mouthed, "Call me!"

Okay. The Frankenstein monster is ready to change back now. Ready! A little help here? Oh, no. it's too late. I'M ALiVE!

CHAPTER SIX

The next day, Gordo walked up to Miranda in the school hallway. "Hey, Miranda, where were you today? We missed you at the debate."

"Doubt that," she said flatly.

"What? We did. Well, I did. Lizzie was a little preoccupied. Claire did a cheer—"

"Of course she did," said Miranda, rolling her eyes.

"Then Claire did a kick and knocked over

Larry's bowl of worms," Gordo went on. "He nearly cried, said it was a conspiracy." Gordo shrugged. "With everyone so distracted by Claire and Larry, all Lizzie had to do was stand there. Out of the three of them, she looked the most normal. Everyone loved her."

"Sounds like Miss Voice of the People was a big hit," Miranda said in a biting tone.

"Miranda?" Gordo knew Miranda was angry with Lizzie, but he didn't expect that she'd totally turn on her.

Miranda didn't see it that way.

"What?" she snapped at Gordo. "The election's tomorrow and Lizzie's blown off everybody to hang with the Drama Club. I hardly even see her anymore and I'm her best friend. She's become a total monster, and it's *your* fault."

"My fault? Lizzie's not a monster, she's a politician."

"You're right, my bad," said Miranda, sarcastic again. "If a politician is someone who lies to people and bosses her friends around, then—you're right—Lizzie's a real politician."

Wow, thought Gordo, Miranda was really burned.

"All right, I get your point," he told her. "I'll have a talk with Lizzie. I'll tell her if she wants to be the Voice of the People, she's got to hang with everybody, not just the Drama Club."

"Okay," said Miranda.

True to his word, Gordo caught up with Lizzie later that day as she was walking through the quad. He explained the issues that Miranda had raised. How she had started out her campaign promising to represent the kids who didn't usually get a voice in student government—the uncool, unpopular, and ordinary kids. But now the only group she seemed to care about was the cool kids in the Drama Club.

". . . So, all I'm saying is, visit some of the club rooms today and remind them that you're Lizzie McGuire, Voice of the People," Gordo advised her. "Do your hair in the braid thingy, and trust me—we'll win this election. Big-time."

Lizzie frowned at Gordo. She didn't like his advice. In fact, she didn't think she even *needed* it anymore—certainly not to win this election.

"I don't think so, Gordo," she replied.

"Why not?"

"Didn't you say I am the Voice of the People?"

"Yeah," said Gordo.

"And didn't you say I have to appeal to everyone?"

"Uh-huh," said Gordo, "but—"

Lizzie cut him off. "Well, aren't I a lot more *appealing* if I hang with the Drama Club over the dorkestra?"

"Well, uh, *no*," said Gordo flatly.

"That's what I thought," said Lizzie. "Bye-bye." And, with that, Lizzie turned around and walked away.

Gordo was stunned. He watched Lizzie cross the quad and join her new Drama Club friends without even glancing back.

"Actually, Lizzie," Gordo murmured, "you're not that *appealing* at all."

When Miranda saw Gordo, she ran up to him.

"Gordo? So how'd it go?" she asked with hope in her eyes.

Gordo shook his head. "You were right, Miranda. I created a monster."

Back at the McGuire house, Matt was home

from school, hangin' in the family room.

Mrs. McGuire walked in the front door, loaded down with grocery bags. She noticed Matt in the big easy chair, talking on the phone.

"Yeah, right," Matt rattled on, "and the day after that . . ."

Thank goodness! Mrs. McGuire thought. My son is finally back to normal!

"Honey, who are you talking to?" she asked.

Matt lifted his chin. "Jasper," he called out. "He's on the moon."

Mrs. McGuire's eyes went wide. Jasper was back? Oh, no.

As Matt continued his side of the phone conversation, Mrs. McGuire felt a chill go through her.

"And then we could go to the moon mall," said Matt dreamily, "and maybe we could get a moon burger, a moon hot dog, and moon fries. . . ."

Mrs. McGuire walked into the kitchen, completely stumped. "On the phone with his invisible friend?" she murmured.

When she passed their second phone, a cordless on the counter, she froze. Eavesdropping wasn't something Mrs. McGuire liked resorting to. But she was a little concerned and *a lot* curious! After all, who wouldn't want to know what an imaginary friend sounds like?

Quietly, she picked up the cordless phone and pushed the TALK button. Matt's voice came over the receiver.

". . . and this make-believe friend thing is working, Doug. My folks are totally conned!"

"What are you gonna ask for next?" Doug asked on the other end of the phone line.

Mrs. McGuire quietly hung up.

So, she thought. Matt was pretending to have a pretend friend to weasel free gifts out of us.

"Okay," she whispered. If make-believe is your game, mister, Mrs. McGuire thought, then get ready to play it *my* way.

CHAPTER SEVEN

Election Day was finally here!

Between classes, students lined up in front of curtained voting booths to cast their ballots for their class president.

As the school day wound down, the three candidates waited patiently in each of their camps.

Claire and Kate were holding court in the cafeteria, surrounded by cheerleaders and jocks.

Lizzie, in shades and a leather jacket, hadn't

even bothered looking for Gordo and Miranda. Instead, she shared take-out coffee with the Drama Groupies in the quad.

Larry Tudgeman was the only candidate still working to earn votes. He'd set up a table near the voting-booth area. Above him his final poster read STILL EATING WORMS.

When the time came to announce the winner, students filed into the assembly room and took their seats, just like they did at lunch— in separate little territories.

The sci-fi kids took one section; the Mathletes took another; the Foreign Exchange Club, yet another.

Lizzie sat in Cool-ville with the Drama Club, still wearing her shades and black leather jacket; Claire and Kate were close by, with their group; and Larry Tudgeman sat alone, surrounded by empty chairs, still holding his bucket of worms.

In the back of the room, Gordo stood next to Miranda. He sighed as he looked over the pathetic scene. "Not only did I create a monster," he said, "but I put her in office."

Up on stage, last year's class president, a popular cheerleader named Holly, tapped the microphone for sound.

"Hello? Hello?" she said. "Okay, it's been really, really, really cool being your class president. And I'm really, really, really bummed that my term is over. But I'm really, really, really psyched to introduce to you your *new* class president!"

As Holly began to tear open the results envelope, Claire handed her pom-poms to Kate. She had to be ready when they called her up to the stage!

Across the room, Lizzie was just as certain she was going to win. She handed her cup of coffee to the Drama Groupie next to her. She had to be ready to go right up when they called *her* name.

Larry just kept staring into his bucket of worms.

Onstage, Holly was all smiles as she finished opening the electoral envelope. Then she looked at the name written on the card inside, and her smile faded.

"Larry Tudgeman," she read, shocked.

All of the kids sitting in the three levels of Dorkdom, and over half the kids sitting in Normal Land cheered and clapped.

Holly grimaced. "I think I'm gonna be really, really, really sick," she said before fleeing the stage.

Both Claire and Lizzie had actually gotten to their feet, expecting to be named president. Now they both just stood there, with looks of horror and humiliation plastered across their faces. They'd been beaten, in front of their entire class. By *worm* boy!

Larry Tudgeman, meanwhile, was still staring into his bucket, convinced he didn't have a chance. Some kid had to tap him on the shoulder and point to the stage.

When Larry awoke from his funk and realized what had happened, he jumped to his feet and threw his arms up in victory.

Then the crowd started chanting. Everyone from the Mathlete, audiovisual, chess, and sci-fi clubs to the dorkestra, gaming geeks, and foreign exchange students started to shout, "Lar-ry, Lar-ry, Lar-ry, Lar-ry!"

As he bounded down the auditorium aisle and up to the stage, more of the crowd went wild. Even some of the jocks had gotten to their feet.

"LAR-RY, LAR-RY, LAR-RY!"

In the back of the room, Miranda and

Gordo exchanged a look of shock—then they joined in the applause.

As Larry began his acceptance speech, Claire felt sick. She dropped back into her seat, afraid she'd either faint or hurl.

Lizzie sunk down slowly, too, listening with a stunned expression.

"Okay," said Larry, "I just want to say, that even though I needed to eat worms to get you guys to notice me, as class president I won't let you down!"

The audience cheered once more.

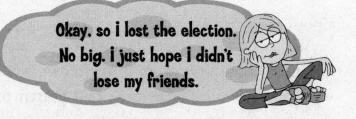

After school that day, the cliques were at their usual Digital Bean tables.

There was Claire's crowd, Veruca's crowd, the Drama Groupie crowd, and then there was Lizzie McGuire, sitting all alone in one corner, drowning her sorrows in a gelato sundae.

Miranda and Gordo approached her.

"Hey," they said.

Lizzie was stunned. "You guys are *talking* to me?" she asked. Nobody else was. The Drama Groupies had considered her a loser and promptly went back to ignoring her.

"You don't deserve it," Miranda admitted, "but . . ."

"*Someone* has to," said Gordo.

"I guess I had that one coming," said Lizzie, looking down. "I haven't exactly treated either one of you like friends lately. I don't blame you guys for not voting for me."

"But I *did*," said Gordo.

Lizzie couldn't believe her ears. "Really?"

Miranda nodded. "Me, too."

"But I was a total monster! I can't believe you guys voted for me after how terrible I was to everyone."

Miranda and Gordo glanced at each other.

"You're my friend," Gordo told Lizzie. "Plain and simple."

"Ditto," said Miranda.

Now that the election was over, Lizzie realized that out of the whole school there were only two votes that she'd really wanted. And she'd gotten them after all.

"Thanks, you guys," she said softly. "That really means a lot to me."

Miranda gestured to the Drama Groupies at the other end of the Bean and asked, "So what happened to your new buds in the Drama Club?"

Lizzie rolled her eyes. "I decided black isn't my color."

A cheer went up near the front door. Lizzie, Gordo, and Miranda looked up to see Larry Tudgeman entering the Bean, high off his win, with more than a few new friends in his posse.

"Larry, Larry, Larry!" the kids in the Bean started chanting.

"Guess, in a way, we kind of won," said Gordo, nodding toward Larry. "I mean, Tudgeman may eat worms, but at least he's not a cheerleader. That's what started this whole thing, remember? I mean, we wanted to stop the popular kids from winning everything."

Gordo is right, Lizzie thought. That's a really good way to look at it. And, who knows, maybe my running was just the thing that split some votes and got Larry the majority after all.

"So, you guys don't totally hate me?" asked Lizzie.

"No. Not totally," said Miranda flatly, but she was smiling.

"Maybe if you got me a cup of *fresh-squeezed* coffee . . . ?" Gordo suggested.

Lizzie laughed. "Coffee is, like, totally gross. What was I thinking?"

"About your *image*, remember?" said Miranda.

"Well, if that ever happens again, I want you guys to promise me you'll stuff me in my locker and won't let me out until I come to my senses."

"Works for me," said Gordo.

"Will do," agreed Miranda.

"Guys!" Lizzie protested.

"We'd never *really* stuff you in your locker," Gordo admitted. "It's too small."

"But maybe a clothes hamper would work," said Miranda.

"Or the janitor's closet," countered Gordo.

"Dumpster?" suggested Miranda.

Lizzie sighed. "I missed you guys."

Whew. Glad that political monster stuff is over with.

By that weekend, things were totally back to normal.

Gordo and Miranda were back at Lizzie's house, hanging out. And when they heard Mr. and Mrs. McGuire laughing their heads off on the backyard deck, they wandered out to see what was so funny.

In the middle of the grassy yard, Matt was standing next to two buckets and a hose. In his hand was a soapy sponge. He moved it in circles, but he wasn't washing anything except the air.

"Aw . . . why don't you go get your friend *Jasper* to help you?" Mrs. McGuire shouted down to her son.

"Matt, I think you missed a spot," called Mr. McGuire.

When Lizzie asked what was up, her mother explained that Matt was trying to con gifts out of them by making up an imaginary friend. So Mr. and Mrs. McGuire decided to make Matt clean an imaginary donkey!

Lizzie loved it! And immediately got into the act. "Yeah, yeah, Matt," she called, "between the ears!"

Matt pouted as he rubbed the air with the soapy sponge.

Trying not to laugh, Mrs. McGuire turned to her husband and asked, "Do you think this punishment is too mean?"

"Mean?" he said, "Nah, 'mean' would be

making him wash an invisible elephant. This is just a donkey."

"Come on, you guys!" Matt complained. "This type of punishment is cruel and unusual."

Everyone just laughed.

In frustration, Matt pointed the garden hose at his parents.

"No," said Mrs. McGuire. "Don't you dare!"

"Matt, you put that down," warned Mr. McGuire. "You're being punished, remember? Put it down, Matt—"

But Matt didn't listen. With one itchy trigger finger, he'd sent a big burst of water his parents' way.

"Matt!" cried Mr. and Mrs. McGuire as they both raced out to grab the hose.

But they didn't really look angry. In fact, the whole thing looked kind of fun.

Laughing, Gordo turned to Lizzie and said, "Next time I get in trouble, I hope *your* parents punish me."

Okay, Lizzie thought, if Gordo wants in on the act, why not make him happy?

She picked up one of the soapy buckets and sloshed it over his head.

The next thing Lizzie knew, Miranda was soaping her face with the big sponge. Then all six of them were laughing and playing, drenching one another with the soap and water and the garden hose.

What a week! Lizzie thought. Larry Tudgeman was the new class president, her brother was forced to wash an imaginary animal, her parents were soaking wet . . . and her best friends hadn't abandoned her. They'd stuck by her through it all.

Yeah, Lizzie said to herself, I may not have won an election, but I haven't lost a thing.

Lizzie
McGUiRE

PART
TWO

CHAPTER ONE

"**L**a, la, la, la!" sang Mr. Escobar.

"La, la, la, la!" echoed the Glee Club.

"Rehearsal better not go late today," Gordo whispered to Miranda between *la-la*s.

The two were standing next to each other on the music room's riser steps, which faced Mr. Escobar's conductor's podium.

Miranda's dark eyebrows drew together at Gordo's complaint. She loved singing, which meant she looked forward to Glee Club after school. What was Gordo's problem?

"I've got three book reports to finish, and a science project to mummify," he explained. "I don't have time for this stuff."

"Well, why'd you sign up then?" asked Miranda.

"Because I need a *non*academic activity on my school résumé to impress charter-school admissions officers," Gordo told her.

Miranda shook her head. She should have known! Gordo seldom did *anything* just for the fun of it anymore. Lately, all his efforts seemed to revolve around a mission to earn five degrees before he turned thirty.

"Okay, people," said Mr. Escobar halting his conductor's baton. "Let's keep our chins high, high, high in the air, and we'll all sound like red-crested warblers!"

"I tell you," Gordo continued, "all this extra work I'm doing—the pressure is killing me."

"And one, two . . ." said Mr. Escobar.

The Glee Club crooned. "'Camptown ladies sing this song—doo-dah, doo-dah!'"

Down the school hallway, Lizzie followed the sound of the singing voices. She paused at the door to the music room, watching Gordo and Miranda chirping their hearts out.

i wonder if the Glee Club is ever going to perform a song that wasn't a big hit during the Civil War.

"Lovely, everyone!" said Mr. Escobar, clapping his hands after the last note was sung. Rehearsal was finally over, and the kids headed for the door.

"Let's practice, practice, practice when we're at home," Mr. Escobar told them on their way out. "And, Gordo, let's keep those 'doo-dahs' a little snappier."

Gordo had to force himself not to roll his eyes in front of his teacher.

"Gordo," said Lizzie, shaking her finger as she walked up to him, "how do you expect to get anywhere in life with sloppy doo-dahs?"

Gordo glared back at his friend.

"Relax," said Lizzie. "It's just a joke!"

"He's kinda stressed," explained Miranda. "Buried under homework and stuff."

Lizzie didn't seem to hear Miranda. She just plowed right ahead with her idea. "You know, I think we should try out for the Fact-Athlon."

Gordo couldn't believe his ears. Miranda had just told Lizzie he was *drowning* in academic work, and her response was to throw a bucket of water on him!

The girl needed a wake-up call. He cupped

his hands around his mouth and yelled, "Hello?"

"Gordo's already getting squashed by all the schoolwork he does," Miranda told Lizzie again. "Why would he sign up for an academic competition that would put even *more* pressure on him? It could kill him."

Lizzie held up a bright yellow flyer. It stood out like a square patch of sun against her hot-pink sparkle top.

"The winners get to go to Miami," she said flatly.

"Miami?!" squealed Miranda. "Oh, Gordo, you've *got* to win this thing for us," she said, shaking him by the shoulders. "*You've* got to study, and *we've* got to win!"

"We'll *all* study. We'll *all* win," said Lizzie. "And *we'll all* go to Miami!"

"Madonna loves Miami," Miranda reminded them.

Gordo thought it over. "The Fact-Athlon *might* be good for my résumé," he admitted. "All right, I'll do it. But we have to do it *together*—and we have to be completely focused."

He held out his hand for the girls to make their pledge.

Miranda placed her hand on top of his. "Completely focused," she promised.

Lizzie's hand joined theirs. "Completely focused," she echoed.

But the image on which she was currently focused had nothing to do with math, science, or history. A lounge chair on the sunny sands of south Florida was more of what Lizzie had in mind!

There! Completely focused.

"Focus, focus, focus, focus!" Lizzie, Gordo, and Miranda chanted.

Their clasped hands bounced up and down like a basketball team about to take the court.

Fact-Athlon, here we come!

CHAPTER TWO

"**O**kay, who was Ulysses S. Grant?" Miranda asked Lizzie.

For the last hour, the two friends had been quizzing each other in the McGuires' living room.

"Okay, okay, okay, I know this," said Lizzie. "He's on the fifty-dollar bill."

"Yeah, but what did he do?" Miranda pressed.

"It had something to do with Abraham Lincoln—" Lizzie guessed.

Miranda nodded. She was getting warm!

"And Lincoln is on the five," said Lizzie, "so that must mean Grant was ten times more important!"

Miranda sighed. Lizzie wasn't *warm* anymore. She was ice-cold wrong.

"He was the commanding Union general of the Civil War," Miranda read from her *People, Places, and Dates in History* book. "Ask *me* something."

Lizzie took the book and flipped a few pages. "Who invented the cotton gin?"

"Oh, shoot. Um . . ." Miranda scratched her head. She knew she had a memory hook for this one. Leaning forward, she began to sing out loud.

Who sings that song? Miranda asked herself, bouncing up and down on the couch cushions.

"Houston, *Whitney* Houston!" she blurted. No, that wasn't the answer, she thought. "Oh, *Eli* Whitney!" she finally shouted—then she slumped back, drained. "I'm running out of memory hooks. This is brutal."

Lizzie sighed. "If our forefathers knew how dull history was going to be, I bet they wouldn't have gone around making so much of it."

"Sorry I'm late," said Gordo, striding into the McGuires' living room. "I was getting you guys some doughnuts."

Miranda frowned. All Gordo seemed to have in his hands were textbooks. "Well, where are they?" she asked.

"Oh, I ate 'em," Gordo said with a shrug. "Yours had coconut," he told Miranda, as if he'd done her a huge favor. "I know you don't like coconut."

"Uh, okay. Thanks, I guess," said Miranda, rolling her eyes. She'd long ago given up trying to figure out, let alone argue with, "Gordo Logic." It was sort of like a giant wave—if you just went along with it, you were much better off.

"So I signed us up for the Fact-Athlon," Gordo told them. "All we need to do now is get a faculty adviser. Every team needs one."

"Oh, let's get Mr. Stoiko," said Lizzie. "He's the smartest teacher in the whole entire school. He's got that huge head."

Gordo sighed. "Kate already got him."

"Kate!" cried Lizzie, seriously annoyed.

Why did snobby she-beasts like Kate always get everything they wanted? Lizzie asked herself. Must be the cheerleader super-powers.

"Don't worry," said Gordo, "we can get Mrs. Trimmer. She's tough, she's smart, and she'll make us study hard."

"Sounds good," said Miranda. "Gordo,

quick—what was Lincoln's Gettysburg Address?"

"Three eighteen Main Street, Gettysburg, Pennsylvania," Gordo answered.

Miranda and Lizzie stared at him.

"Just a joke," he said, with a shrug.

"That's not a joke," said Lizzie. "What does a cannibal call a phone book?"

Gordo and Miranda stared at her.

"A menu!" said Lizzie. "Now *that* is a joke!"

Gordo and Miranda just kept staring. They were not amused.

But Lizzie was. That joke always cracked her up!

As Lizzie, Miranda, and Gordo went back to quizzing one another, Lizzie's little brother, Matt, and his silent best friend, Lanny, headed into the McGuires' kitchen.

Mr. McGuire was lying on his back, fixing the drain under the sink. Mrs. McGuire was standing next to him, handing him different-sized wrenches.

"Hey," Matt asked his mother, "do we have any musical instruments?"

"My old cymbals from marching band," said Mrs. McGuire.

"No good," said Matt. "Lanny and I are starting a band. We're livin' the dream. And you can't play a blistering rock-and-roll anthem on the cymbals."

"Well, how about my old guitar?" suggested Mr. McGuire, pulling his head out from under the sink. "I used to be in a band myself, you know."

"*You?* Were in a *band*?" asked Matt.

Mr. McGuire nodded with pride.

Matt and Lanny didn't just burst out with laughter. They burst out with *hysterical* laughter. Lanny was beside himself, and he pounded on the butcher block as Matt sank to the floor.

"Yeah, I was in a band," repeated Mr. McGuire, a little irritated by their reaction. "Me and cousin Ree-Ree and his buddy, Stucco. We were called Midnight Sam and the Love Patrol."

Mrs. McGuire's eyebrows rose. She remembered that band. They'd had shaggy haircuts, worn silk shirts and gold chains, and played disco music. Unfortunately, Ree-Ree's keyboard had short-circuited at one of their performances. Mr. McGuire didn't like to talk about how things had really gone downhill for the band after that.

"Hey, I'll have you know, son, we rocked," declared Mr. McGuire.

Mrs. McGuire suppressed a snort.

Mr. McGuire shot her a warning look. It was bad enough his son was laughing at him. He wasn't about to put up with his wife laughing, too.

"Sorry," she said, holding back a grin. But,

unfortunately, Matt and Lanny still couldn't keep from laughing themselves silly.

The next day, Lizzie, Gordo, and Miranda sat at their desks, waiting for Mrs. Trimmer to arrive and class to start.

"Mrs. Trimmer wanted me to work out a study schedule," Gordo told them, passing around his notebook while they waited. "I figure we'll put in an hour each day in math, science, history, and English."

"I guess I'll just have to get by on three hours of sleep," said Lizzie, looking over Gordo's schedule.

i cannot possibly study four extra hours a day and still have time for the important stuff. (You know, talking on the phone, watching TV, doing my nails.) This is really going to be a sacrifice!

"I'm giving up eating dinner and talking to my parents," Miranda declared as she eyed the schedule. "But it'll all be worth it when we go to Miami. We're totally going to win with Mrs. Trimmer."

"Mrs. Trimmer has left the country," announced Mr. Digby Sellers as he strode into the classroom. "I'll be substituting for her while she's gone."

Lizzie's and Miranda's jaws dropped. Even Gordo sputtered.

"B-but, Mr. Dig," said Gordo, "she's supposed to be our adviser for the Fact-Athlon."

"Oh, I got your back on that one," said the substitute teacher.

"*You're* going to be our adviser?" Lizzie asked a little skeptically. She wanted to get this straight right now. Miami meant too much to her.

"Hey, I was good enough to tutor Christina Aguilera in Spanish," said Mr. Dig.

Lizzie's eyes widened.

"I was good enough to tutor the governor of Michigan in economics—" he continued.

Miranda's eyebrows rose.

"I was good enough to tutor Ben Affleck about Pearl Harbor."

"You taught all those people?" asked Lizzie.

"Oh, no—they wouldn't let me," said Mr. Dig. "But I was *good* enough. And if I'm good enough for them, I'm good enough for you. Meet me back here at five o'clock. We'll start with math."

Miranda and Lizzie looked at each other. Even Gordo, who usually followed this weird type of logic, was dubious on this one. "This should be interesting," he said with a sigh.

Well, thought Lizzie, we do need an adviser. And Mr. Stoiko is taken. Why not at least give Mr. Dig a try?

CHAPTER THREE

After school that day, another sort of tryout was about to begin in the McGuires' back-yard.

Matt and Lanny set up a card table and two chairs. Matt checked his wristwatch and then his clipboard of names.

"Hey, guys," called Mr. McGuire from the deck. "What're ya doing?"

"Well, Lanny says that all the best bands

have more than two people, so we're having auditions for a third member," explained Matt.

"Ah," said Mr. McGuire. "So, there's gonna be lots of kids playing instruments *real loud* all afternoon?

"Uh-huh," said Matt.

"Uh-huh," said Mr. McGuire. Then he turned and yelled into the house. "Hey, honey, I'm gonna head down to the office for the rest of the afternoon!"

The boys and girls started arriving soon after Mr. McGuire left. They auditioned on every sort of instrument, too: clarinet, trumpet, congo drums, xylophone.

One of the last kids to audition was a violin player. She looked about six years old, tops. Played like it, too. "Great, babe," Matt told her. "We'll call you, okay?"

Finally, a drummer auditioned. He was a

bit older than the other kids—like *thirty-five years* older!

But Matt wasn't the sort of kid who engaged in age discrimination, so he had the man assemble his drum kit on the McGuires' deck.

"Name, please," Matt asked.

"Reggie. Reggie McGreggor," said the man.

"He's a bit old to be a rock star," Matt whispered to Lanny. Then Matt looked over his résumé.

"Says here you've played with Linda Ronstadt, James Taylor, Steely Dan, John Lennon . . ."

Matt looked at Lanny.

Lanny shrugged.

"Never heard of 'em," said Matt. "Okay, let's see what you got."

Reggie played a blistering drum solo. Matt and Lanny nodded.

"Congratulations, Reggie—you've got yourself a gig."

"Thanks, guys. Thanks for the break," said Reggie. Suddenly, a cell phone rang. "Oh, excuse me," Reggie said as he pulled the cell from his pocket and put it to his ear. "Hello? Dad, I got the gig!"

While Matt and Lanny were putting together their rock band, Lizzie and Miranda were putting together their Fact-Athlon study aids.

"Protractor, compass, and calculator," Lizzie said, as she fished the items out of her locker.

"Aw, look at Lizzie studying," Kate taunted as she walked by. Geek-boy Larry Tudgeman and fellow cheer-snob Claire Miller were with her. Mr. Stoiko, their adviser, trailed behind in his tweed suit, a thick book in his hands.

"You guys really think you can beat us?" Kate asked.

Tudgeman was practically swaggering. "You guys have less of a chance than Marc Antony's fleet at the battle of Alexandria in 12 B.C.," he said. "It was a *Tuesday*."

"You guys," Claire whined to her teammates, "we've got no time to waste. We've got to study. Study!"

"Study! Study!" Miranda and Lizzie echoed, making faces at their departing opponents.

"Mark Anthony, the singer?" Miranda whispered to Lizzie, still trying to figure out what Tudgeman meant.

Lizzie rolled her eyes. She still couldn't get over the fact that Kate had asked *Tudgeman* to be on her team. Normally, Kate would have rather been caught wearing clothes from her mother's 1970s wardrobe than seen standing next to him. Even if Tudgeman *was* the smartest kid at Hillridge, he was also a total geek—far from the ultracool crowd Kate usually hung with.

On the other hand, a trip to Miami was at stake. And Kate was ferocious about winning *any* competition she entered. Larry Tudgeman just might be her big-brained secret weapon.

Who cares, anyway, thought Lizzie. Miranda and I have a secret weapon, too.

Just then, Lizzie noticed her secret weapon lumbering down the school hallway. He didn't look much like a secret weapon at the moment, though. He looked more like a very large cardboard box with two legs sticking out.

"Is it safe?" Gordo asked from behind the huge box of books he was carrying.

"Yeah," said Lizzie, "go straight."

Miranda opened the classroom door.

"Yeah, okay," she told him, "now turn right," she said as Gordo turned sharply and bounced off the wall. "No, not so early!"

"Yow!" he yelled from behind the box.

"Okay, now turn around," Miranda directed, after Gordo—and the box—finally made it through the classroom doorway. "Now go left. No, not *your* left!"

Thud.

"Whoa!" Gordo cried as he slammed into the teacher's desk.

"Is that Gordo back there?" asked Mr. Dig, who was sitting behind the desk, and trying to peer behind the huge box.

"I checked out every math book the library had," Gordo announced, still trying to balance the heavy weight.

"And we have our compasses, rulers, protractors, and everything," said Lizzie, dropping them onto Mr. Dig's desk.

"Good, good," said Mr. Dig. "Get rid of it all."

"Why?" asked Gordo. "What are we gonna study with?"

"These." Mr. Dig tossed something to Gordo, who had to drop the box of books to catch it.

"Those are *cards*," said Miranda, her tone just a *tad* cranky.

"*Very good*, Miranda," said Mr. Dig, putting her in her place in record time. "If we need you to identify any other objects in the Fact-Athlon, *you're* our go-to girl."

Taking back the deck of playing cards, Mr. Dig opened the pack and began to shuffle them.

"So, what are we gonna do? Study math by playing *poker*?" asked Lizzie.

"Of course not," said Mr. Dig. "What kind of bughouse idea is that? We're gonna play *blackjack*!"

Lizzie's eyes widened.

"Grab some chairs," said Mr. Dig.

Lizzie was game. She pulled up a chair.

Gordo just stood there, mouth agape for a second. "Maybe Mrs. Trimmer didn't *explain* the Fact-Athlon to you. But it's intense. We have to *study*."

"We are," Mr. Dig told Gordo. "We're just gonna do it a little differently. Look, we're gonna learn things by *doing* them. And if you play blackjack, you learn math: addition, subtraction, probability, ratios."

"I think we should study the old-fashioned way," said Gordo. "You know, where you read books, and you memorize facts—"

"—where you turn yourself into an old worried man," Miranda finished for him. Mr. Dig had won her over. She'd pulled up *her* chair. The only holdout now was Gordo.

"I am *not* an old man," snapped Gordo.

But he finally pulled up a chair, too. "Ow!" he cried as he sank down. That box had really messed him up! He rubbed his sore back. He may not have *been* an old man. But he was starting to feel like one!

"I think Mr. Dig's way could work," Lizzie told Gordo. "I think it could really work well."

Mr. Dig smiled.

Lizzie smiled back.

"Hit me, dealer!" she said brightly.

Mr. Dig flipped a card, and began their first math lesson—Digby Sellers style.

CHAPTER FOUR

The Mr. Dig study sessions continued every day after school: math, history, science, and English.

On the day Team Lizzie was supposed to begin studying history, Mr. Dig told Lizzie, Gordo, and Miranda to wait at a table in the quad.

The three nearly lost it when their teacher strode up to them, dressed in Elizabethan garb, complete with silk stockings and ruffled collar. He was also carrying a basket of food.

"English history," announced Mr. Dig, gesturing to the basket. "Grab thee a turkey leg and eat it fast, 'cause we didn't have refrigeration in the sixteenth century, and the only way to preserve this is to cake it with salt."

To make his point *real* clear, he grabbed a saltshaker and shook!

The next day's study session was on science.

Books were out. Hands-on work was in. So they all met in the chemistry lab.

"Okay, we start with H_2O," Mr. Dig told Lizzie, who wore a white lab coat, goggles, and thick black rubber gloves.

At Mr. Dig's direction, Lizzie poured water into a glass beaker.

"And then we add bicarbonate of soda," Mr. Dig told Miranda, who spooned the white powder into the beaker.

"And that creates carbon dioxide!" said Mr. Dig as the mixture began to bubble.

When math day came around again, Team Lizzie was really cookin'.

"Okay," said Miranda, examining her cards. "I know there are at least twelve more face cards in the deck, which means there's a two-to-one ratio of face cards to spot cards, so I'm going to split my eights, so I can double my cookies."

She then put the two eights side by side in front of her, with a small stack of Oreo cookies (that she was using as gambling chips) on each eight.

Wow, thought Lizzie. Blackjack has totally expanded Miranda's mathematical mind.

Mr. Dig nodded. Miranda was really getting it!

By the next session on English history, Team Lizzie had gotten into the whole "living history" thing, too. Like Mr. Dig, they'd put on Tudor costumes, assumed roles of historical characters, and chowed down on a sixteenth-century-style meal.

Gordo took the part of Henry VIII. Miranda pretended to be Anne Boleyn, Henry's wife. And Lizzie played the part of Jane Seymour, Anne's lady-in-waiting.

"Anyone seen much of the peasants lately?" asked Lizzie, as she nibbled at a piece of cheese.

"Saw them just today," said Miranda, eating a bunch of grapes.

"Oh. And how are they?" asked Lizzie.

"Muddy. Y'know, wallowing in the muck and whatnot," said Miranda, making a face.

Then she turned to Gordo, who was gnawing on a turkey leg.

"By the way, my liege," she said, "I hath failed to produce thee a male heir for the throne."

"No matter," said Gordo. "I'll just break away from the Church of Rome, start the Church of England, have your head lopped off, and marry that saucy wench." He gestured to Lizzie.

"'Kay!" said Lizzie, through a mouthful of food as she smiled and licked her fingers.

On their next science lab day, Mr. Dig taught them all about mixtures. When they were almost finished for the day, he told Gordo to pour soda into a beaker.

"Then we add a sucrose compound and a thickening agent," said Mr. Dig. Lizzie poured in chocolate syrup and milk.

"We shake it all up," said Mr. Dig.

Lizzie put a lid on the beaker and shook it.

"And that creates . . . an egg cream!" said Mr. Dig, picking up the beaker and taking a sip of the famous Brooklyn drink.

"L'Chaim!" he exclaimed, and Team Lizzie laughed.

Not everyone was laughing, though.

While Lizzie, Gordo, and Miranda were doing their hands-on learning, Kate, Tudgeman, and Claire sat at the same table in the quad, day after day. Under the stern gaze of Mr. Stoiko, they studied nothing but names and dates in textbooks.

On their next English history study day, Gordo, Lizzie, and Miranda decided to taunt their opponents. Together, they ran through the quad in their Elizabethan getups, sprinkling flower petals and playing music they'd learned from the Tudor period.

"Do you believe those jerks?" snapped Kate, brushing a fistful of potpourri off her textbook.

"No time to talk!" scolded Claire, who was sitting alongside her. "Study. Study!"

Kate frowned and scratched her collarbone. Tudgeman, who was sitting on the other side of her, noticed a rash creeping up Kate's neck.

"Uh, you got some sort of Snakewoman from Mars thing going on your neck there," he told her.

"It's a stress rash from all this studying!" Kate snapped. "Leave me alone!"

"Would you guys *quit* distracting me?" yelled Claire, who was so stressed out that she began chewing her French manicure.

Maybe Lizzie, Gordo, and Miranda were lucky that they didn't get stuck with Mr. Stoiko, after all!

"Time to understand physics," Mr. Dig told Team Lizzie on another science study day.

He'd asked them to carry a bag of groceries up the steps at the far end of the grassy quad.

"Bodies of unequal weight fall at the same speed," he explained.

Lizzie dropped a watermelon at the same time that Miranda dropped an egg. They fell with the same speed, making a really cool smash on the concrete below.

"Ooh, cool!" said Lizzie. "Watermelon omelette."

As they dropped more vegetables, Mr. Dig explained how Galileo influenced Sir Isaac Newton, who'd later developed the laws of gravity.

Lizzie was diggin' it. Who knew science could be this cool? she thought.

By the next math study day, Team Lizzie was red-hot.

"Hit me!" cried Lizzie.

Mr. Dig slapped down a card.

"Thirteen. Hit me."

Mr. Dig slapped down another card.

"Boo-ya! Twenty-one!" cried Lizzie, throwing up her arms in victory. She'd calculated the mathematical probabilities and outcomes perfectly.

She was *so* ready for the Fact-Athlon—or Vegas—either one.

Cash me out. i'll be at the buffet.

"That's a ridiculous name!" Matt yelled at Lanny. "I don't want to call our band the Lanny and Matt Band. What kind of name is that? How could you come up with that?"

In the kitchen, Mr. and Mrs. McGuire heard their son's angry voice. They followed it to the backyard deck.

"Hey, what's going on out here?" asked Mrs. McGuire.

"We can't agree on a name for the band," Matt explained. "I want something thought-provoking, something that says we're all about the issues."

"Well, what do *you* want to call it?" asked Mrs. McGuire.

"Spoink," said Matt, holding up a note-book with the name *Spoink* spelled out in thick red letters.

"Well, maybe you guys should focus more on rehearsing," suggested Mr. McGuire, "and the name'll take care of itself."

"You're right, Dad," said Matt. "We gotta be all about the music."

As he picked up his guitar and Lanny hoisted a stand-up bass, Matt glanced over at his middle-aged drummer.

Reggie had apparently been through this sort of dysfunctional band scene before. During the entire argument, he'd just been sitting quietly at his drum set, drinking coffee and reading the paper.

"Count us in, Reggie," Matt called.

"One, two, three—" Reggie counted off four beats and the band started up.

Mr. and Mrs. McGuire wanted to like the band's music. They really did. But to their ears, it was just noise. Loud, horrible noise. Neither Matt nor Lanny could keep time. Reggie tried to help them out, but then Matt started singing. Only it sounded more like shouting:

"'HOW MANY TIMES HAVE I HEARD YOU COMPLAIN?'" he bawled into the microphone. "'ONCE. TWICE. THREE. FOUR. FIVE. SIX . . .'"

Mr. and Mrs. McGuire were stunned at how very bad it sounded. After a long, horrifying two minutes, Mr. McGuire bailed.

"I'll be at the office!" he yelled over the noise.

Across town, at Lizzie's school, the Hillridge Fact-Athlon was about to begin.

The stage in the assembly room looked like the set from a game show. Two tables had been placed at either end of the stage, one for each team.

Between the tables rose the moderator's podium. And behind everything stood a lighted scoreboard—on loan from the P.E. department.

Kate, Tudgeman, and Claire had gotten to their table early so they could get in some last-minute practice.

"Fifth Amendment?" barked Tudgeman, his face twitching.

"Um, protection against self-incrimination," answered Kate, scratching her neck rash, which had now spread to her chin and cheek.

Lizzie, Gordo, and Miranda sauntered to their own table, cool, calm, and confident.

Gordo gave a relaxed wave to Kate. "Greetings, wench. Good fortune and fair time of day."

Kate scratched her rash, and Gordo made a face. That thing looked *nasty*. "Ew," he said.

"Shouldn't you weirdos be out playing dress-up, or something?" cracked Tudgeman, as one eye began to blink uncontrollably.

"Listen, twitchy," said Miranda, "you guys are going down faster than a watermelon dropped off a building."

"Yeah," said Lizzie. "While you guys were *studying* stuff, we were *living* it."

After Team Lizzie took their seats, Mr. Escobar addressed the rather thin crowd of teachers and students. Since the competition was being held after school on a Friday, very few people had actually made the effort to stay and watch.

Mr. Escobar didn't act like he cared, though. He was as enthusiastic as ever. "Thank you for coming, everyone, and welcome to the twelfth annual Fact-Athlon!"

The small crowd applauded.

"Our first category is English History."

Lizzie nearly jumped for joy. That was a Team Lizzie specialty!

From the audience, Mr. Dig looked pleased, too. He gave them a thumbs-up.

Lizzie was feeling so confident, she actually caught Kate's eye and said: "Fare thee well, Kate. We've come to bury you, not to praise you."

Alas, poor Kate. Har-har-har!

Mr. Escobar pulled out his index cards and read the first question. "Who commanded the British fleet at the Battle of Trafalgar?"

Miranda snapped her fingers. Lizzie scratched her head. Gordo closed his eyes. But none of them had the answer.

Buzz!

Kate hit the buzzer. "Lord Horatio Nelson," she said.

"Correct," said Mr. Escobar and immediately read the next question. "Name the competing factions in the War of the Roses?"

This time, Claire hit the buzzer.

"The Lancasters and the Yorks," she said.

"Correct," said Mr. Escobar. "Who signed the Magna Carta?"

Now Tudgeman buzzed in. "King John. In the year 1215. At Runnymede."

"Correct," said Mr. Escobar.

"Uh-oh," mumbled Lizzie. Distressed, she

looked at her teammates. Then at Mr. Dig. He looked as confused as she felt.

We studied for weeks, she thought. And we learned so much! Why can't we *answer* anything?

CHAPTER SIX

As the Fact-Athlon dragged on, the electronic scoreboard counted up points.

Team Kate: 12.

Team Lizzie: 0.

"Moving on to the American Revolution," said Mr. Escobar. "What year did the Boston Tea Party occur?"

Buzz!

"December 16, 1773," said Tudgeman, his eye still twitching.

On the other side of the stage, Team Lizzie was freaking.

"Why didn't we get that one?" Miranda whispered.

"'Cause we didn't study dates and places and times!" said Gordo.

"I know what the colonists *felt*, but I don't know *when* they felt it." Lizzie groaned. "We need questions about turkey legs."

"This is massively stinkful," said Miranda.

"What year did Abraham Lincoln sign the Emancipation Proclamation?" asked Mr. Escobar.

Buzz!

Miranda just couldn't take it anymore. She'd hit the buzzer.

"He signed it so that abolition would become an actual issue of the Civil War," she answered, "and to show that he was confident in the Union Army after the Battle of Antietam."

That answer was excellent, thought Lizzie.

It captured Miranda's complete understanding of the significance of the historical event.

But Mr. Escobar made a pained face. "Mmmm. We're looking for the *date*," he told her.

"Oh, right," said Miranda awkwardly. "The date, I see. . . . Pass."

Buzz!

"September 22, 1862," Kate rattled off.

That's it, thought Lizzie. This competition isn't about learning—it's about memorizing! And I'm not going to sit here and watch my friends be humiliated like this—not to mention, *myself.*

"Here's the plan," Lizzie whispered to her team. "Gordo, you fake being sick. Miranda, you turn on the fire sprinklers, and we're gonna get out of here."

"Get real," said Gordo. "We just have to *focus.* We can do this."

Buzz!

Tudgeman buzzed in for yet another answer. "Edward Jenner discovered the smallpox vaccine."

"Oh, for pity sake." Gordo groaned.

From there, it all pretty much went downhill.

Mr. Escobar asked a question. And someone on Team Kate answered it.

"What is the square root of pi?"

Buzz!

"One point nine eight three two four," said Tudgeman.

In the audience, Mr. Dig was shaking his head. He looked totally disturbed.

The whole thing started taking on a kind of surreal quality for Lizzie. She could barely hear the questions anymore.

Buzz!

"Charles Dickens in 1849," said Kate.

"Correct," said Mr. Escobar.

Buzz!

"1812," said Claire.

"Correct!" said Mr. Escobar.

The scoreboard racked up point after point for Team Kate. Nineteen, twenty, twenty-one, twenty-two—

Buzz!

"Missouri Compromise," said Tudgeman.

Buzz!

"July 20, 1969," said Claire.

Buzz!

"Ring-tailed lemur!" cried Kate.

Finally, the scoreboard read twenty-five to nothing, and even Gordo had had enough.

"Oh, my heart!" he yelled. "Aggghh!"

"Gordo, are you okay?" cried Lizzie.

Gordo clutched his chest in exaggerated agony, then pitched himself onto the table.

The audience watched, horrified. No one

noticed Miranda slip away to trigger the fire sprinklers.

"C'mon, c'mon, c'mon!" Miranda whispered to her friends from the stage's side exit as chaos erupted in the assembly room.

Lizzie and Gordo bolted from the stage a second before water rained down, drenching Team Kate and that evil, awful scoreboard.

Back at the McGuire house, Mr. and Mrs. McGuire were having about as much fun as Lizzie.

"Do we have any aspirin?" shouted Mr. McGuire over the noise in the backyard. He began frantically searching through the kitchen cabinets.

"*You* got a headache, too?" yelled Mrs. McGuire, joining his search.

"No," said Mr. McGuire. "I just think they'd make good earplugs."

Suddenly, the noise stopped, and Mr. and Mrs. McGuire sighed with relief.

"Hey," called Matt, bounding into the kitchen. "I need some root beer for Lanny, and some coffee and antacid for Reggie McGreggor."

Mr. and Mrs. McGuire exchanged a meaningful look. Both of them wanted to say the same thing. Mrs. McGuire spoke first.

"Matt," she began gently, "your dad and I are thinking that maybe this band thing just isn't working out. I mean, you guys rehearse a lot—"

"A *lot*," echoed Mr. McGuire.

"And you're not getting much better," finished Mrs. McGuire.

"Are you saying we should quit?" asked Matt.

"No," said Mrs. McGuire, suddenly worried about hurting her son's feelings. "No, no, no—"

"Well, *yes*," corrected Mr. McGuire. He was way more concerned with his eardrums at the moment than how his son felt.

Matt narrowed his eyes at his parents. "Haven't you guys always told me that if you really love something, you should stick with it, no matter how long it takes?"

"Yeah, you know what?" said Mrs. McGuire. "We *have* always said that, but the thing is—" she was now considering her own eardrums, not to mention her sanity. "We were wrong."

"Dead wrong. We see that, now," agreed Mr. McGuire.

"Our band isn't giving up," said Matt, incensed. "Today's Friday. And by the time we have our backyard concert on Sunday, we're gonna be laying down some *insane* tuneage." He turned to go, then stopped to add one more thing. "And we don't need your root beer."

Mr. McGuire looked like he was about to cry. He turned to his wife. "The office is *closed* on Sunday."

After fleeing the Fact-Athlon stage, Lizzie, Gordo, and Miranda ran out of steam pretty quickly. All three slumped down in the school stairwell, feeling totally defeated.

"*That* didn't go well," said Gordo.

The *Titanic* didn't go well. But *this* was a disaster. All we did was talk like Old English weirdos and eat turkey legs.

A door slammed and three pairs of feet clattered down the stairs.

Wet and twitching, Kate, Tudgeman, and Claire approached Team Lizzie.

"Well, it looks like you didn't bury us," Kate said, gloating.

"We buried *you*," said Claire. "I've got to hand it to you. It's not often that students do so bad that their *teachers* quit."

"What?" asked Lizzie. "Mr. Dig's quitting?"

"That's what he told Mr. Escobar," said Kate. "Well, see you in Miami. Oh, wait—I guess we won't!"

Lizzie barely heard Kate's final swipe. She suddenly didn't care about Miami. Or about winning. Neither did Miranda or Gordo. All they could think about was the awful news that Mr. Dig was quitting—and Lizzie couldn't help feeling responsible.

CHAPTER SEVEN

On Sunday, a few neighborhood kids and an eighty-year-old man sat in the folding chairs that were set up in the McGuires' grassy backyard.

Reggie's drum kit was set up on the deck. Matt's guitar and Lanny's bass were resting upright on instrument stands. And an amplifier and mike were at the ready.

It was time for Matt's rock concert, and

Mr. and Mrs. McGuire took their seats, dreading what was about to happen.

Lizzie had refused to give up her day to sleep in. She'd even put plugs in her ears the night before so she wouldn't be disturbed.

"Did you warn the neighbors?" Mrs. McGuire asked her husband. She was nervous. She could already envision the complaints.

"I promised them I'd mow their lawns and give them fifty bucks if they didn't call the cops," he told her.

Matt, Lanny, and Reggie strode through the house's back door and onto the deck "stage" as if they were entering a stadium filled with adoring fans.

Matt wore a crazy feather vest, gold chains, and clip-on earrings. Lanny sported orange pants, a sleeveless black shirt, and goggle shades. Reggie wore a black glitter shirt—possibly left over from his days of disco dancing.

Reggie took his seat at the drum set and waved to the old guy in the audience. "Heya, Dad. Thanks for coming," he said.

Reggie's dad gave him a thumbs-up.

Matt strapped on his guitar and threw a disgusted glance at his parents. "See? *Reggie's* dad is supportive."

Mr. McGuire sighed. Fifty bucks and a mowed lawn promised to every neighbor on the street and all he got was attitude. Would he never catch a break?

"I got a gig to play," Matt told them.

"Rock on," said Mrs. McGuire sweetly. She wasn't looking forward to the massive headache awaiting her. But it *was* her only son. The least she could do was cheer him on.

Matt walked up to the microphone. Reggie and Lanny readied their instruments.

"One . . . two . . . three . . . four—" Matt counted off, and suddenly the band launched into a rockabilly tune that blew everyone away.

What the heck had happened? The band wasn't just good. It was amazing!

As Reggie whaled on the drums, Matt sang his heart out. His fingers flew up and down the frets of his guitar. And Lanny was playing his bass like a pro, sinking down to the ground to play it on his knees, then riding it like a horse, then spinning it around and dancing with it.

Mr. and Mrs. McGuire just stared, open-mouthed.

Mrs. McGuire turned around in her seat. "That's my baby, with the guitar!" she told Reggie's dad, filled with pride.

"And that's *my* guitar," said Mr. McGuire, just as proudly.

The band continued to play. Neighbors, still wearing bathrobes, wandered into the yard to see what sounded so great. Then the crowd started dancing.

Finally, the band finished and took a bow to cheers and applause.

Reggie's dad gave his son a big thumbs-up.

"Hey, good job," Mr. McGuire told Matt as the crowd headed home.

"Matt, Matt, honey, that was incredible!" gushed Mrs. McGuire.

"Oh, thanks," said Matt with a shrug. "I thought we were all right."

"All right? What's next?" asked Mr. McGuire.

"What do you mean?" asked Matt, packing up the guitar.

"Where are you guys going to play next? Are you going to get an agent?"

"Nah," said Matt. "We're through with this."

"What? Why?" asked Mrs. McGuire.

"Because we've done it. It's history." Then Matt and Lanny exchanged a look—their special way of communicating.

"Lanny has a good point," said Matt. "We've never done snowmobile racing. C'mon, Lanny, let's get that into the works."

A moment later, Matt and Lanny were gone.

Mr. and Mrs. McGuire looked at each other and shrugged. Who could figure out Matt logic—and, more important, why even try?

CHAPTER EIGHT

When Monday morning came around, Lizzie, Miranda, and Gordo found Mr. Dig. He was in Mrs. Trimmer's classroom, packing his things into a cardboard box.

"Hey, Mr. Dig," said Lizzie.

"Hey," he said, but there was no energy in his voice.

"We heard you were leaving," said Miranda.

Mr. Dig nodded dejectedly. "Well, I let you guys down, didn't I?"

Lizzie watched him continue his packing. What could she do? What could she say? She had to think of something.

"You can't leave, Mr. Dig!" she blurted.

"Why not? I'm a terrible teacher. You didn't learn anything from me."

"I wouldn't exactly say we didn't learn anything," argued Lizzie.

"I learned how to play 'Greensleeves' on an autoharp," Miranda pointed out.

"And I learned that it's good to split nines if the dealer has a five or six showing and there are no other tens on the table," offered Gordo.

"Actually, I learned a lot," said Lizzie. Now that she thought about it, she totally did. "Like the Middle Ages smelled terrible, and you were lucky if you lived to be thirty 'cause there was *so* not any hygiene."

"And it didn't matter that Galileo proved Earth isn't the center of the universe. That meant nothing unless the political powers would let him *tell* people," said Miranda.

"And that wasn't gonna happen," added Lizzie, "'cause then *they'd* be out of a job."

Mr. Dig looked surprised. And sort of pleased. He'd actually stopped packing and was really listening to them.

"I always busted my tail for school," Gordo said sincerely. "I never knew it could be *fun* before."

"Or interesting," agreed Lizzie. "Yesterday, I got a book on Queen Elizabeth the First out of the school library."

Queen Elizabeth was fat, bald, and looked like a clown. You can look it up!

"We have a school library?" asked Miranda.

Lizzie poked Miranda in the ribs.

"Well," said Mr. Dig, "I guess I didn't do such a bad job, after all." Then he smiled that sly Digby Sellers smile. "In fact," he said, "sounds to me like you should be *thanking* me."

"Well, I wouldn't go overboard," said Lizzie. "We *did* want to go to Miami."

"Yeah," said Gordo. "We'll thank you if we survive the gloating Kate does when she comes back from Florida next week."

One week later, Team Kate returned from Miami.

Lizzie, Gordo, and Miranda were hanging out in the school hallway when they saw Kate, Claire, and Tudgeman walking toward them.

Here we go, thought Lizzie. She braced herself for massively obnoxious gloating, followed by stories of sun, sand, and tropical Slurpees.

But Team Kate didn't look like they were going to gloat. They didn't even look happy. In fact, they appeared to be in *agony*.

Kate was covered in welts.

Claire was hobbling on a crutch.

And Tudgeman was red as a lobster.

"What happened to you guys?" asked Lizzie.

"I got bitten to death by sand fleas!" snapped Kate.

"I stepped on a stupid sea urchin," snarled Claire.

"I got so sunburned, my teeth hurt," said Tudgeman, who was barely able to move his blistered lips.

As the three bitter "winners" hobbled on down the hallway, Mr. Dig came up behind a giggling Lizzie.

"*Thanks*, Mr. Dig," she told him. Miranda and Gordo thanked him, too.

Their Fact-Athlon adviser had not only opened their eyes to new ways of learning, he'd obviously saved them from the perils of paradise.

Mr. Dig smiled. "Don't mention it."

Don't close the book on Lizzie yet!
Here's a sneak peek at the next
Lizzie McGuire story. . . .

OH, BROTHER!

Adapted by Jasmine Jones
Based on the series created by Terri Minsky
Based on a teleplay written
by Douglas Tuber & Tim Maile

Lizzie McGuire was sitting at the kitchen table, struggling to write her history report. *Why do we even have to learn about this* stuff? Lizzie wondered as she took notes on the chapter. I mean, it's all totally over.

And speaking of totally over . . . Lizzie thought, as she watched her brother practicing his latest magic trick. He was flapping a scarf. After a minute, it turned into a cane. Lizzie rolled her eyes.

Ever since Gammy McGuire had sent Matt a magic kit for his birthday, he had been going crazy with the tricks. And he was driving everyone else crazy, too. Well . . . everyone except for Mom and Dad, Lizzie realized, watching her parents as they calmly sliced vegetables for dinner. So I guess that only leaves me, she thought. But still—isn't that enough?

"Wow!" Matt said as he stared at his cane. "That was amazing. Hey, Lizzie, you wanna see a magic trick?"

Lizzie looked down at her paper. "No."

"For my next illusion," Matt announced, completely ignoring Lizzie's wishes, "the famous Floating Ball." So, Matt was making a grapefruit-sized silver ball float around under a scarf, Lizzie thought. Big deal. Dad makes a *real* grapefruit disappear every morning at breakfast.

"It floats on top of the scarf! It hides behind the scarf! It zooms through the air!" Matt announced.

The ball flew forward and conked Lizzie on the head. "Ow!" she cried, grabbing the ball and scarf and chucking them into the garbage. "It flies into the trash!" she shouted.

"Dad," Matt whined, "Lizzie threw my trick away!"

"Lizzie, don't throw your brother's trick away," Mr. McGuire said in a bored voice as he kept on slicing and dicing.

Matt flashed Lizzie an evil grin. "Ha!" He

said as he fished the ball out of the wastebasket and carried it triumphantly to Lizzie. He thrust it into her face. "Now, kiss it and say you're sorry," Matt commanded.

Lizzie shoved the ball away. "Get out of my face, Cactus-head."

"Mom, Lizzie called me Cactus-head!" Matt complained.

"Lizzie, don't call your brother a cactus-head," Mrs. McGuire said automatically.

Fine—he's a cactus-*brain*, Lizzie thought. "But I'm trying to do my homework and he won't stop bothering me with his stupid magic tricks," Lizzie cried.

"They're *not* stupid," Matt insisted as he pulled a deck of cards from his magic kit. "Here, pick a card—" He fanned the deck in her face.

Matt has got to stop getting all up in my face, Lizzie thought. Furious, she took a card and slipped it into her pocket. There, she thought, whine about that.

Sure enough. "Liz-zie!" Matt wailed.

"Liz-zie!" his sister repeated in a mocking tone.

"Kids . . ." Mrs. McGuire said in a warning voice.

Matt reached for the card, but Lizzie held it away from him. "I need the card to do the trick!" Matt insisted.

"I can do a better one with it—" Lizzie snapped. She slipped the card out of her pocket and tore it up. "Ta-da!" she said, tossing the shredded card into the air. "I turned it into confetti!"

Matt glared at her. "Well, well," he said, "how about I turn this into confetti—" Matt yanked a pink scarf out of his sleeve.

"That's mine!" Lizzie cried. "And I told you to stop going into my closet!"

"It wasn't *in* your closet," Matt said in his most annoying know-it-all voice. "It was in your underwear drawer."

"That's it," Lizzie said through clenched teeth. She grabbed Matt's shirt and yanked him forward. "I'm telling Dad what *really* happened to his sunglasses."

"Fine," Matt said smoothly. "I'll tell Mom what you were talking to Miranda about on the phone last night. At *eleven thirty,*" he added, putting extra emphasis on the way-past-lights-out time. "'Ooooh,'" Matt squealed, mocking Lizzie's voice, "'Ethan Craft is soooo cute. I just want to hug and kiss him all day long!'"

Lizzie flashed him the Look of Death, then lunged at him. Matt dodged away, squealing like a stuck pig, and Lizzie chased after him.

"*Aaaaaaaagghhhh!*" Matt shouted as Lizzie finally grabbed him.

"FREEZE!" Mrs. McGuire shouted.

Lizzie stared at her mother. Then she looked down at Matt. Okay, so this looks kind of bad, Lizzie realized as she stood there, holding Matt upside down by the ankles.

"Let go of me!" Matt shouted, flailing like a cat that had fallen into the toilet bowl.

"Lizzie," Mr. McGuire said slowly, "put Matt down and step away from your brother."

Lizzie set Matt down and took a giant step away from him. "He started it!" she shouted, just as Matt shouted the same thing, only about Lizzie.

Grrr, Lizzie thought, glaring at her little brother.

"I don't *care* who started it!" Mrs. McGuire snapped. "You kids have got to stop this constant bickering."

"What is it with you guys?" Lizzie's dad

demanded. "You never used to fight like this when you were younger."

That's because Matt didn't know how to talk, Lizzie thought sulkily.

"You used to really take care of each other," Mr. McGuire pointed out. "And that's what a family is—people who love each other and take care of each other."

Lizzie sighed. Her father had a point. She forced herself to smile and slung her arm around Matt, who squirmed. That's okay, Lizzie thought generously, I can forgive him. "You're right, Dad," Lizzie said sincerely. "Sorry, Mom."

Dad's right. Matt's family. We've gotta have each other's backs. We've gotta be all about love.

Besides, Lizzie thought as she tightened her grip on her brother, it's not like Matt really did anything so horrible.

Except go in my underwear drawer. . . !

On the other hand, the little rat STOLE MY SCARF!

"She's pinching me!" Matt griped.

"He's standing on my foot!" Lizzie cried.

"Well, at least you're not standing on *my* foot," Matt shot back, "you weigh a ton!"

"Oh, you little weasel—" Lizzie growled, "I'll teach you to make fun of me!"

"You don't have to teach me—" Matt quipped. "I already know how to!" He strutted around, fluffing his prickly-pear hair.

"'Ooooh, I'm Lizzie,'" Matt cooed, batting his eyes. "'Notice me, Ethan! Notice me, Ethan. Ethan, Ethan, Ethan!'"

Lizzie swung at him, and Matt took off, up the stairs. She raced after him, shrieking. No jury would convict me! Lizzie thought as she pounded up the stairs. Everyone would understand!

Mr. and Mrs. McGuire stared after their children for a moment. Finally, Mrs. McGuire turned to her husband and asked the question that was on both of their minds: "Potatoes or stuffing?"

Sorry! That's the end of the sneak peek for now. But don't go nuclear! To read the rest, all you have to do is look for the next title in the Lizzie McGuire series—

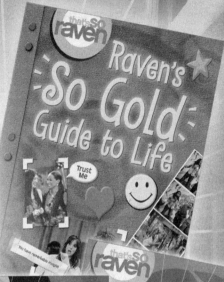

Groove to the sound of all your favorite shows

Disney Channel Soundtrack Series

Disney's
Kim Possible
TV Soundtrack

The Cheetah Girls
TV Soundtrack

Lizzie McGuire
TV Soundtrack

Pixel Perfect
Soundtrack

Also, look for...

- **The Proud Family TV Series Soundtrack**
- **That's So Raven TV Series Soundtrack**

Collect them all!

Wake up.
Go to school.
Save the world.

W.i.t.ch.

Will · Irma · Taranée · Cornelia · Hay Lin

The magic of friendship

The new book series · Make some powerful friends at www.clubwitch.com